The MAGIC BRUSH

The MAGIC BRUSH

Illustrated by Y. T. Mui
Adapted from the original folktales
by Robert B. Goodman and
    Robert A. Spicer
Edited by Ruth Tabrah

An Island Heritage Book

Produced and published by Island Heritage Limited
Norfolk Island, Australia

Copyright © 1974 Island Heritage Limited
ALL RIGHTS RESERVED
Library of Congress Catalog Number **74-80513**
ISBN Trade **0-8348-3032-9**
This edition first published in Japan

For the Island Heritage distributor in your area,
please write or phone:

Island Heritage Limited (USA)
Editorial Offices
1020 Auahi St., Bldg. 3
Honolulu, Hawaii 96814
Phone: (808) 531-5091
Cable: HAWAIIBOOK

Engraving, printing, and binding by
Leefung - Asco Printers Ltd. Hong Kong

ISLAND HERITAGE

EDITORS
Robert B. Goodman
Robert A. Spicer

ASSOCIATE EDITOR
Carol A. Jenkins

CONSULTING EDITORS
Ruth Tabrah
Rubellite K. Johnson
Frances Kakugawa
George A. Fargo
Jodi Belknap

CONSULTING ART DIRECTORS
Yoshio Hayashi
Nella Hoffman
Herb Kawainui Kane

To David Andrew
and Maile Lisa. . .

Long ago in China there ruled a greedy Emperor.
His treasures and lands were beyond counting -
but always he wanted more. Under him, even
the rich became poorer. And for the poor,
each day was a new struggle to stay alive.

In one small village
there lived a poor boy
named Ma Lien.
Every day
he trudged off
to gather firewood
for the few coins
he needed for food.
He had no family,
no friends,
no time for play.
He had
only his dream –
to become a painter
of pictures.

Rich boys on their way to the village art
school made fun of Ma Lien.
"Poor boys can't go to school,"
they taunted.

How Ma Lien envied them.
To learn to put what their eyes
saw into colors, shapes,
into brush strokes
on fine paper - that
was Ma Lien's dream.

Whenever he could, Ma Lien would climb into a tree to watch the teacher give the rich boys their art lessons.

One day he was discovered.

"The beggar boy! He spies on us!"

Ma Lien jumped from the tree
and ran, but the art teacher
caught him.

"You are a thief!" shouted
the teacher. "Trying to learn
without paying is as bad as
stealing." And he beat on
Ma Lien's head with a string
of coins.

"Painting is not for a poor boy like you!
Go! Get to your wood gathering!"

Sadly, Ma Lien went on his way.
"How could he learn to paint if no one
would teach him?"

That evening, after his supper
of plain rice and tea, Ma Lien sat
watching the neighbor's chickens. In
his mind, he drew each detail of feather
and spur and beak.

"No!" thought Ma Lien. "I will
not give up my dream.
I can be a painter of
pictures."

The next day, pausing at a forest pool,
Ma Lien was overwhelmed
by the beauty that he saw.

"I must draw it!" cried Ma Lien.

And so, with a twig for his brush and a smooth patch of dust, Ma Lien set to work.

He forgot his woodgathering, forgot hunger, forgot time.

He practiced drawing everything he knew.

Day after day
Ma Lien would practice.
One day, while resting,
he fell fast asleep.

In his sleep, he dreamed
that an old man came and spoke to him.

"You have worked hard, Ma Lien,
to make your dream come true.
Here is a magic
brush that will help
you paint whatever you wish.
But remember, use it
only for the good
of the people!"

And with those words,
the old man disappeared.

When Ma Lien awoke,
a golden brush
was in his hand.

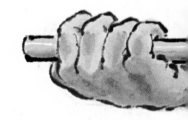

Ma Lien raced home. "A brush!
My own brush!"
This day, he traded his firewood
not for food, but for paper
and a cake of ink.

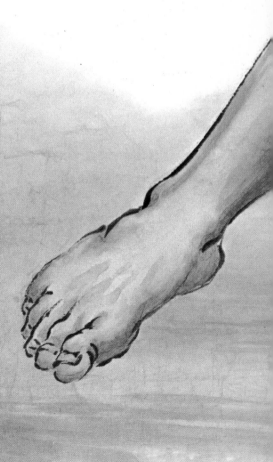

At the mountain pool,
Ma Lien had learned with his
eyes and heart every motion
and fin and scale of the fish there.

"I will paint a fish with my
magic brush," thought Ma Lien.

As he finished the tail,
the fish suddenly leaped
from the paper into a nearby
water jug.

"It is indeed a magic brush,"
gasped Ma Lien. "With my
last stroke the fish has
come to life!"

Ma Lien remembered that in his dream
the old man had instructed him to use
the magic brush for the good of the people.

"I will!" "I will!" vowed Ma Lien.

For the people
of his village,
Ma Lien magically
painted into life
buffalo to plow
the fields and
water wheels to
irrigate them.
These he gave
freely to those
in need.

The villagers
were overjoyed with
their good fortune.
Everyone prospered.
Ma Lien was happy.

One day in the marketplace,
Ma Lien painted a giant crane.

The villagers were so fascinated
they failed to notice one of the
Emperor's soldiers among them.

As Ma Lien added the final brush
stroke, the crane rose from
the paper and flapped
noisily into the air.

Astounded, the soldier
raced to tell the Emperor
what he had seen.

Soon, the Emperor's men arrived
in the village with orders to bring Ma Lien
and his magic brush to the royal court.

It was a long road from the village
to the Imperial City of Peking.

"Ma Lien!" greeted the Emperor.
"We have heard of your great power.
Now you will have the honor of painting
for your Emperor."

"All my life I have wanted to see a
real dragon breathing fire and
smoke. All my life I have wanted
to see a real phoenix. Paint them
for me with your magic brush!"

Ma Lien
did not like
the greedy Emperor.
And so
instead of a phoenix
and dragon,
he painted an ugly cock
and a huge toad.
On his last brush stroke,
the cock flew up
and pecked the Emperor.
The ugly toad croaked
and jumped about.

The Emperor was furious.

"To the dungeon with this impudent beggar boy!" he commanded.
"Give me his magic brush. I shall paint what I please for myself."

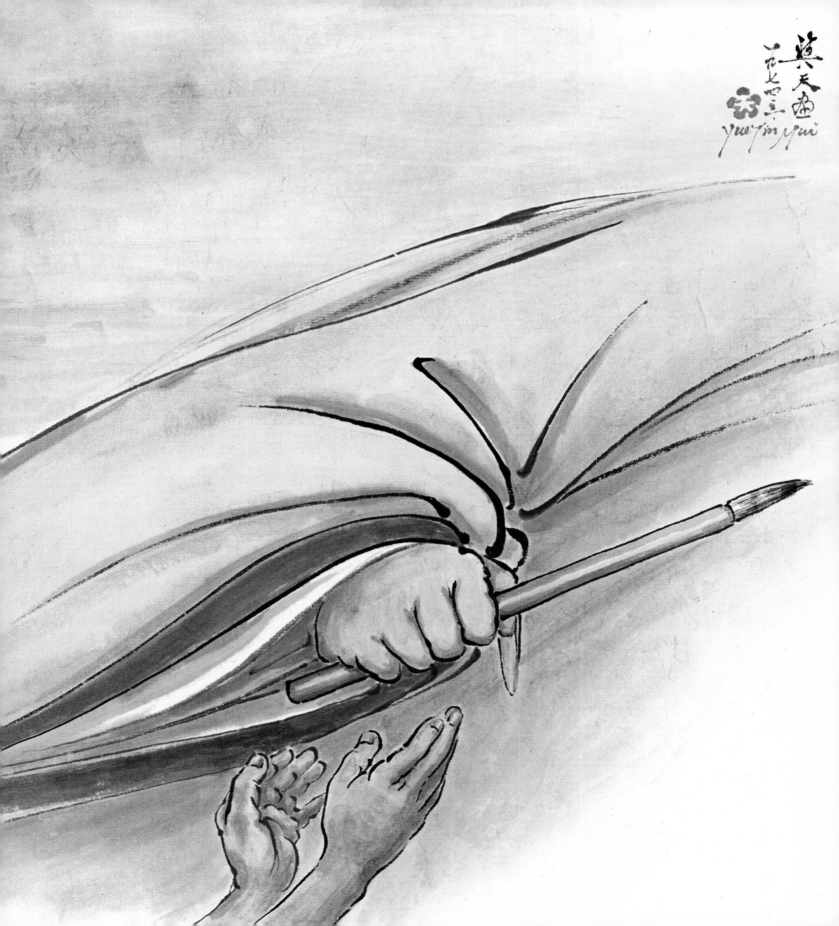

As if it knew the hand
that held it, the brush
would not
work its magic
for the Emperor.

His painting of a
golden mountain
became falling rock.
His golden dragon,
a snake that tried
to bite him.

The greedy Emperor
barely escaped
with his life.

The Emperor was a determined man. He had Ma Lien released from the dungeon.

"Paint for me and I shall make you rich. I shall give you my daughter, the Princess, as your bride."

"I paint only for the good of the people," said Ma Lien.

"Then paint an ocean!" commanded the
Emperor.

"Yes, that is a good idea," answered Ma Lien.
"I will paint an ocean,
your Celestial Majesty."

Ma Lien's brush created the white crest of
waves breaking on a blue-green sea.

The Emperor was pleased. "Excellent!"
he said, "Excellent!"

"Now paint me a ship, Ma Lien. Paint me a ship as I would go for a ride on this beautiful ocean of yours!"

With the magic brush, Ma Lien
painted the most elegant royal ship
the Emperor had ever seen.

"Magnificent," said the Emperor.
"Now paint me an ocean breeze!"

"You mean wind, your Majesty?"
asked Ma Lien.

"Yes wind!" said the Emperor.

Ma Lien obeyed.

He painted a wind so strong and fierce that
the Emperor and his ship were swept far out
to sea, and never seen again.

And so it was
that a new
Emperor came
to rule over China,
an Emperor who
was kind and
compassionate
and wise.

The story of
the magic
brush was
celebrated
throughout
the four corners
of the Celestial Kingdom.

And Ma Lien? He returned to his village
and grew to manhood, a painter of pictures.
His wealth was in treasures more real
than gold and silver - family, friends,
and the art that was his life.

Introducing Other
Folktales, Myths and Legends
from Island Heritage

Seven Magic Orders
Chinese Folktale
80 pages, all color, *$4.95*

Momotaro
Japanese Folktale
64 pages, all color, *$4.95*

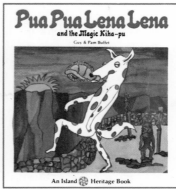

**Puapualenalena and The Magic
Kiha-pu,** Hawaiian Legend
78 pages, all color, *$4.95*

Kamapua'a
Hawaiian Legend
88 pages, all color, *$4.95*

Kahala, Where the Rainbow Ends
Hawaiian Legend
56 pages, all color, *$4.95*

Felisa and The Magic Tikling Bird
Filipino Folktale
68 pages, all color, *$4.95*

Urashima Taro
Japanese Folktale
68 pages, all color, *$4.95*

The Secret of Beaver Valley
An American Fable
100 pages, all color, *$4.95*

The Richest Man In Babylon
Babylonian Fable
64 pages, all color, *$4.95*

**Makaha, The Legend of the Broken
Promise,** Hawaiian Legend
64 pages, all color, *$4.95*

Issunboshi
Japanese Folktale
68 pages, all color, *$4.95*

The Magic Brush
Chinese Folktale
64 pages, all color, *$4.95*

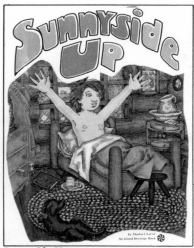

Acknowledgements

The Editors of Island Heritage
are especially grateful to
Mr. Ernest Yu of Hong Kong for
his suggestion of "The Magic
Brush."

We also wish to acknowledge
Mr. Edward R. Bendet, Mr.
Martin I. Rosenberg, and
our friends at Pacific Phototype, Inc.
Ron Gandee, Elizabeth Owen and
Penny McCracken.